HELPING OUT

BY GINA AND MERCER MAYER

Published by FastPencil PREMIERE
307 Orchard City Drive, Suite 210, Campbell CA 95008
Premiere.FastPencil.com

JUST LEAVE ME ALONE

BY GINA AND MERCER MAYER

Sometimes I don't want to be with anyone.
I just want to be left alone.

I wanted to play video games by myself,
but my sister came into the room.
I said, "I want to be alone."
She said, "I want to sit here."

I went to the kitchen to get a snack. Mom came in to feed my little brother. I had to hold him while she fixed his food.

I went to the garage to be alone.
Dad was there. I had to help
him carry some boxes.

I went to my sandbox. My sister was there. I said,
"I want to play in the sandbox by myself."
She said, "It's my sandbox, too."

So I got on my bicycle. My neighbor
came over and asked if he could
ride with me.

I asked Mom if I could go for a walk.
My little sister said, "Can I come?"
Mom said, " He wants to be alone."

My little sister didn't walk with me.
She followed me.

When I was going up to my room to be alone, someone knocked on the door. It was my grandma and grandpa.

I had to visit with them.

When they left, I went outside to play basketball.
My sister went, too. I said, "Leave me alone."
She said, "I want to watch."

So I sat on the porch and read my book. But my dog kept jumping on me and I couldn't read. I said, "Just leave me alone!" He didn't understand.

I went to my room. I was finally alone.
Then Mom called, "You and your little
sister need to set the table for dinner."

I didn't want to have dinner. I just wanted
to be left alone. I yelled, "I want everyone
to just leave me alone!"

Dad said, "If you really want to be alone, stay in your room." And he closed the door.

Then I was really alone.

I could hear everyone downstairs having dinner. I felt so lonely. I wanted to have dinner with my family.

I went downstairs.
Dad said, "I thought you wanted to be alone."

I said, " I only wanted to be alone for a few minutes."

Being alone is all right when you want to be alone.
But being with your family is a lot more fun.

I'M SORRY

BY GINA AND MERCER MAYER

Whenever I do something wrong.
I just say, "I'm sorry."

I knocked my sister off her bicycle by accident.
I said, "I'm sorry."

I left my sister's jump rope at the park.
I said, "I'm sorry."
We had to walk all the
way back to get it.

I used my brother's blanket for my
Super Critter cape. It got dirty when I
was playing outside. I said, "I'm sorry."

When I was playing hide-and-seek with my sister, I got tangled in the curtain and pulled it down. I said, "I'm sorry."

When I was trying to reach my favorite book, I knocked all the other books down. I said, "I'm sorry." Mom helped me put them back.

Mom said, "The baby is napping , so please play quietly."
I forgot to play quietly. I woke the baby.

I said, "I'm sorry."
Mom said, "Go play
outside."

I didn't know the baby's bedroom window
was open. "I'm sorry, Mom," I said.

When I was playing football,
I got tackled in Mom's
garden. I said, "Sorry!"

Mom and Dad asked me to close my bedroom window when it rained, but I forgot. I said, "I'm sorry."

I didn't empty my pockets before Mom washed my pants. I said, "I'm sorry."
Mom said, "That's what you said last time."

I really wasn't sorry that I forgot to clean my room. I hate to do that.

But I really was sorry
when I stepped in a
mud puddle with
my new shoes…

and that I didn't
wash my hands
before I picked up
the baby's bunny.

41

But I was especially sorry
that I left the top off my ant farm.

At dinner, Dad put some broccoli on my plate. I said, "I'm sorry, I don't like broccoli."
Dad said, "I'm sorry, you have to eat some anyway."

43

I was kind of messy when I was taking a bath. I said, "I'm sorry."
Dad made me clean up the bathroom.

After I took apart my sister's dollhouse, I couldn't put it back together. I said I was sorry. My sister called Mom.

While Mom fixed the dollhouse, I was supposed to watch my little brother. Oops!

I said, "I'm sorry, Mom."
Mom said, "Sometimes saying
'I'm sorry' just isn't good enough."

48

I didn't know that.

If saying "I'm sorry" isn't good enough, I guess I'll just have to be more careful.

JUST SAY PLEASE

BY GINA AND MERCER MAYER

My teacher said that good manners are important. She also said that everyone in our class could use a little help with good manners.

We made a good manners chart. We took turns telling the teacher what to put on it.

I said, "Cover your mouth and nose when you sneeze." My dad told me that.
The teacher said that was a very good one.

The class went over everything
on the list, one by one.

Remember to say, "Please."
I remember to say please
when I want to stay up
past my bedtime.

Remember to say,
"Thank you."
I always remember to
say thank you when I get
what I want.

56

Take turns.
I take turns most of the time.
But sometimes it's so hard to wait.

Don't interrupt when
someone is talking.
I guess that's why
Mom gets so mad
when I talk to her
while she's on
the phone.

Share.
I didn't know sharing was good manners. I wonder if my sister knows about that.

If you bump into someone or step on someone's toe, say, "Excuse me."

I guess that keeps people from getting mad at you.

Don't put your elbows on the table.
I didn't know *elbows* were bad manners.

Say you're sorry when you do something wrong.
I'm not too good at that.

Put your napkin on your lap at the dinner table.
I thought that was just so silly.

My teacher said that we would go over the list every morning so that we could tell her what we did to show good manners.

I thought that was neat. I decided to try to
have good manners right away.

When I got home, I ran in the front door and
knocked my sister down. I said, "Excuse me."
That didn't help. She cried anyway.

I went to tell Mom.
She was talking on the phone. I forgot
I'm not supposed to interrupt when
someone is talking.
So I said I was sorry.

Boy, was she surprised! She didn't even get mad at me for interrupting.

When Dad came home, I asked him to play a
game with me. He said he was too tired.

I said, "Please."
But he still said, "No"
I guess good manners
don't always work.

65

At dinner I put my napkin on my lap.
My sister asked me why.
I said, "Because it's good manners."

Then my napkin fell on the floor.
My sister said, "You dropped your good
manners."

When Mom passed the rolls, I remembered
to say thank you.
Mom said my teacher was doing a great job
teaching us good manners.

68

I even remembered to keep
my elbows off the table.
Dad didn't, though.

After dinner I let my sister color my homework picture. I thought it was nice of me to share my homework.

70

The next day at school, we went over the good manners list. We each told how we used good manners.

Only one other critter in my class had better
manners than me.
She got a big sticker that said I HAVE GOOD MANNERS.
It was cool.

I'm working really hard to remember my
good manners because my teacher gives out
a sticker every day.

And I love to get stickers.

JUST A GUM WRAPPER

BY GINA AND MERCER MAYER

My teacher said that we have to take care of the Earth because it takes care of us.

I didn't know that.

My teacher said the Earth gives us a place to live...

air to breath...

water to drink...

and food to eat.

I guess the Earth really does take care of us.

My teacher said that we also have to take care of the things that the Earth gives us— so that there will be enough for everyone.

I told my Mom and Dad. They said
my teacher was smart.
I said, "I want to be careful and
take care of the Earth."
They said that was a good idea.
So we thought of some things
we could do to help.

We try really hard not to throw trash on the ground. One day I had to remind my sister. She said, "It's just a gum wrapper."
I said, "What if everybody in the whole world said that?"
She picked it up.

We turn off the lights when
we're not in the room.
When I'm brave, I even
turn off my night-light.

I still have to remind Dad to turn
off the TV when he is sleeping.

I never forget to turn off the water
in the tub anymore. Sometimes
I still forget about the sink.

85

We only buy cleaning stuff that doesn't harm the Earth. And we try to buy things in containers that can be used again.

At home we have special places to put plastic, glass, paper, and cans so that they can be recycled. Recycling is one of the most important things we can do to help.

PLASTIC

GLASS

PAPER

CANS

But sometimes I get mixed up.

Now Mom hangs the wash on the clothesline instead of using the drier. I have to be careful not to knock the clothes down.

We used cloth diapers for my little brother
instead of the kind you throw away. That's
good for the Earth, but it's kind of messy.

A truck comes to bring clean diapers
and take the yucky ones away.

My sister and I try to remember to close
the refrigerator door when we're finished.

HOLD THE PICKLES!

Mom's been trying to get us to do that
for a long time.

When we take our empty bottles and cans
to the recycling place, we get money for them.
Mom lets us spend some of the money.
We buy lots of neat stuff.

At school we made a chart to see which family did the most to take care of the Earth in one week. My family won.

There was a class party, and my whole family came. That was fun. I was really proud. I was even proud of my sister.

Then we planted a tree by the playground.
The teacher said it was my special tree for
doing such a good job.

That made Mom and Dad really happy.

I still have a lot to teach my baby brother
about taking care of the Earth.